For Rosie and Raffi – N.K.

EGMONT

We bring stories to life

First published in Great Britain 2011
by Egmont UK Limited
239 Kensington High Street
London W8 6SA

Text and illustrations copyright © Nicola Killen 2011
The moral rights of the author/illustrator have been asserted

ISBN 978 1 4052 5424 3 (Hardback)
ISBN 978 1 4052 5425 0 (Paperback)

1 2 3 4 5 6 7 8 9 10

www.egmont.co.uk

A CIP catalogue record for this title
is available from the British Library

Printed and bound in China

46323/1/2

Nicola Killen

Fluff and Billy

do everything together!

EGMONT

I'm climbing up! said Fluff.

I'm climbing up! said Billy.

I'm sliding down! said Fluff.

I'm sliding down! said Billy.

AAAAAAAAAAA

AAAAAAAAA

screamed Billy.

AAAAAAAAAAAHH!

screamed Fluff.

AAAAAAAAAAAHH!

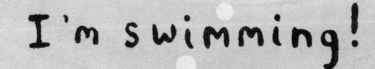

I'm swimming!

said Fluff.

I'm swimming!

said Billy.

I'm running over here!

said Fluff.

I'm running over here!

said Billy.

I'm jumping up!

said Fluff.

I'm jumping up!

said Billy.

I'm rolling a snowball!

said Fluff.

I'm throwing a snowball!

said Billy.

OUCH!

cried Fluff.

I'm not talking to you!

said Fluff.

I'm not talking to you!

said Billy.

Fluff said
nothing.

Billy said
nothing.

I'm tickling your tummy!

said Fluff.

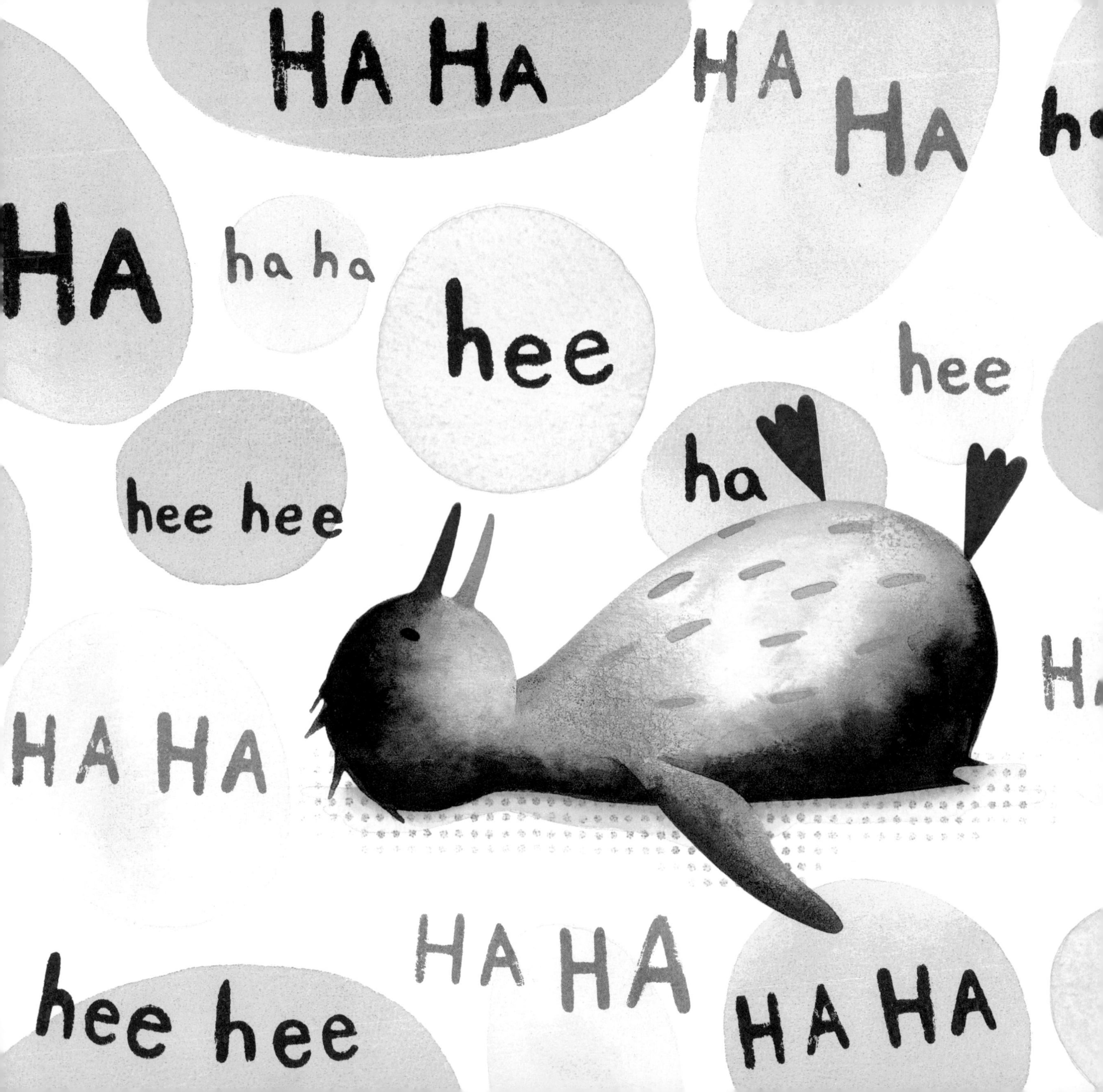
HA HA
HA
HA
HA
ha ha
hee
hee
hee hee
ha
HA HA
HA HA
hee hee
HA HA

laughed Fluff and Billy...
...together!